ESCAPE TO CANADA

by Rob Arego

illustrated by Bob Novak

D1301774

Strategy Focus

As you read, pause and **summarize** each part of the story to help you understand what has happened so far.

HOUGHTON MIFFLIN   BOSTON

Key Vocabulary

arming providing with weapons

drilling doing exercises to become good soldiers

fierce harsh and forceful

just honorable and fair

kin relatives; family

peered looked at with concentration

rebels people who are against the government

skirmish a small, short fight between enemies

skittish nervous and jumpy

Word Teaser

Change two letters of **skirmish** to tell how you might feel before a big test.

It was 1776. The American Revolution was just starting. Everywhere, people were getting ready for war. Men were arming themselves with rifles. They were drilling, or doing exercises to become good soldiers. They wanted to fight for freedom from British rule.

But some people did not want freedom from Britain. These people were called Loyalists.

This is a true story about what happened to one Loyalist family.

Benjamin Ingraham was a Loyalist. He lived in what is now New York State with his wife and young children. His daughter, Hannah, was just four when he left home to join the British army.

Hannah was sad to say goodbye to her father. She didn't know it would be seven years until she saw him again. Her family would face many problems during those long years.

Hannah's neighbors were rebels. That means they were against the British. They were angry at her family. The rebels passed a new law. The law let the rebels take away the Loyalists' land and belongings. They took the Ingrahams' farm. The family was left with almost nothing.

Hannah knew the rebels were not being just, or fair. But there was nothing the Ingrahams could do.

All through the war, life was hard for Hannah and her family. They were afraid of their rebel neighbors. The fighting made them nervous and skittish.

Worse still, Hannah never heard from her father. She feared he had died in a short fight, or skirmish, with the rebels.

Then, in 1783, Hannah's father came home. The war was finally over! But the Ingrahams were not safe yet.

The rebels had won the war. Benjamin Ingraham told his family to pack up their belongings. They were going to Canada. Canada still belonged to the British. There, the Ingrahams and other Loyalists could live without fear of the rebels.

The family prepared for their trip. They loaded food and other supplies onto wagons. These supplies would help them survive their first winter in Canada.

Hannah was now 11 years old. She brought a diary along, too. She wanted to write about her family's journey.

The Ingrahams started their trip. It was early fall. The days were getting cold. The family had to reach New York City in time to catch a ship to Canada. They arrived just in time for the last boat of the season!

The ship reached Saint John, Canada, in early October of 1783. From the ship's deck, Hannah peered out at her new country. She saw snow falling on the ground. The air was cold and wintry.

The months ahead were hard for the new settlers. They lived in tents. They had very little food. Many people got sick and died. Hannah and her family struggled through the fierce winter. It was a miserable time, but they all survived.

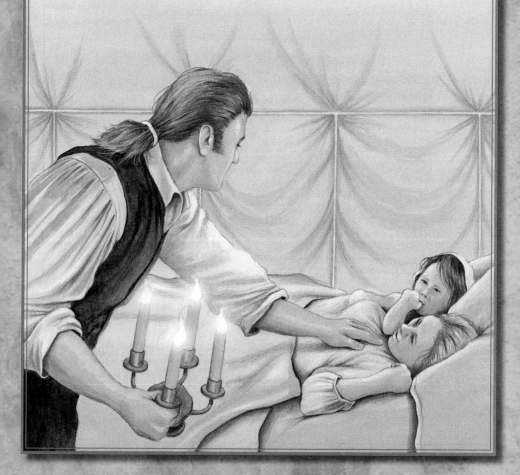

This photograph of Hannah Ingraham was taken in 1860.

Hannah and her kin, or family, lived in Canada for the rest of their lives. They had found a new home where they could live in peace. We know this because Hannah's diary survived her journey too, and lived on long after her.

Putting Words to Work

1. Name some of your **kin**.

2. How were the laws passed by the **rebels** unfair?

3. Describe a situation that might make you feel **skittish**.

4. Describe some of the things an army might do while **drilling**.

5. **PARTNER ACTIVITY:** Think of a word you learned in the text. Explain the meaning to your partner and give an example.

Answer to Word Teaser

skittish